GHOST MOON

Adapted by Lauren Forte
from the episode "Ghost Moon" written by Greg Johnson
for the series created by Sascha Paladino
Illustrated by Patrick Spaziante

 A GOLDEN BOOK • NEW YORK

 Published in the United States by Golden Books, an imprint of Random House Children's Books, a division of Penguin Random House LLC, 1745 Broadway, New York, NY 10019, and in Canada by Penguin Random House Canada Limited, Toronto, in conjunction with Disney Enterprises, Inc. Golden Books, A Golden Book, A Little Golden Book, the G colophon, and the distinctive gold spine are registered trademarks of Penguin Random House LLC.
randomhousekids.com
ISBN 978-0-7364-3717-2 (trade) — ISBN 978-0-7364-3718-9 (ebook)
Printed in the United States of America
10 9 8 7 6 5 4 3 2 1

Miles and his sister, Loretta, are playing hide-and-seek. Even though it's dark in the living room, Merc, their robo-ostrich, easily finds their hiding spot.

SQUAWK! Merc says when he sneaks up on them.

Miles giggles. "You found us, Merc! Good boy."

"I can't believe what a master he is at this game," says Loretta.

Just then, the family receives a message from the Tomorrowland Transit Authority.

"Hello, Callistos," says Admiral Watson. "We need you to go to Phantasmos, the moon that orbits the planet Fraylak. A crew was building a charging station, but they left after they heard a ghost!"

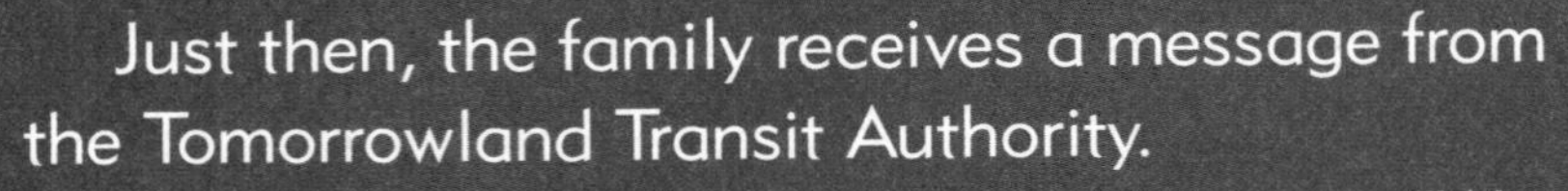

"Since you are the bravest crew in the TTA," continues Admiral Crick, "we want you to go there to check things out. Good luck. Over the ghost moon and out."

Leo and Phoebe, Miles' parents, are ready for the mission.

"Well, it looks like we're going on a good old-fashioned ghost hunt," Leo says.

"I sure hope we catch one!" Miles says excitedly.

Whoooooosh! Their ship, the ***Stellosphere,*** blasts through space. When the Callistos get close to Phantasmos, they take the ***StarJetter*** down to the moon's surface.

As soon as the Callistos exit the StarJetter, they are surrounded by light-flies. Merc doesn't like them.

"It's okay, Merc," Miles tells him. "Light-flies are just curious. They won't hurt you."

Soon the family sees the charging station in the distance. Just then, they hear a ghostly moan.

Who-OOOO-oooo!

"Okay," says Loretta, "if there were such thing as ghosts, they would sound just like that."

"The sound is coming from that direction," Leo says, pointing.

Everyone hops into the scout rover to get a closer look.

"Hey, what's that?" asks Phoebe as they drive toward a large, shadowy figure.

"It could be a giant ghost," Miles suggests hopefully.

But as the fog shifts, they see it's just a big tree covered in moss.

"Awww, craters," says Miles, disappointed.

Suddenly, the ground under the scout rover crumbles. The rover slides rapidly down the mountain . . .

. . . then soars up a dirt ramp and flies through the air. Finally, it crash-lands in a swamp.

"Ghost hunting is ***SPACE-TACULAR***!" Miles shouts.

Who-OOOO-oooo!

The Callistos hear another ghostly moan as some four-eyed creatures pop out of the water.

"They're marsh frogs," Loretta reports, checking her **BraceLex**. "It says here that they can copy any noise."

SQUAWK! says Merc.

SQUAWK! SQUAWK! SQUAWK! repeat the marsh frogs.

"That solves the mystery," says Loretta. "The crew heard the toads making the ghost sounds."

"But the frogs just repeat stuff. They must have heard the ghost sounds first," says Miles. "We need to keep looking."

The Callistos continue through the mist. They hear the moaning again, and this time they see an eerie light floating above a chasm!

"It *is* a ghost!" cries Loretta.

"I don't know—it sounds kind of electronic," Miles says.

"Like a siren that's losing power!" says Phoebe.

Loretta checks her BraceLex again. “The shape is a help symbol that’s used on the planet Worlia,” she says. “I bet someone crashed down there! Okay—I found a news report about a lost Worlian ship. It says the pilot’s name is Nuala, and she’s been missing since yesterday!”

The family notices that the help symbol has disappeared and the siren has stopped.

"It's going to take a while to search this whole chasm," says Leo.

"Not with the master of hide-and-seek—right, Merc?" asks Miles.

Merc squawks in agreement.

"Okay, buddy, let's find that ship!" Miles shouts.

Merc scans the area with his special triangulation vision, but he doesn't spot the missing ship.

"Maybe it sank in the mud?" Miles suggests.

At that moment, a swarm of light-flies passes them, making the swamp bright enough for Miles to see a metal wing sticking out of the water.

"It's the ship!" shouts Miles. "It's a good thing light-flies are curious."

"We've got to rescue the pilot, Mom!" Miles says.

"We will!" Phoebe assures him.

Leo quickly uses the scout rover to tow the stranded spaceship out of the mud.

Phoebe rushes to open the hatch.

"Nuala?" she calls. "We're the Callistos. You're going to be okay."

"Thank you for saving me!" Nuala says, relieved.

"Let's get you home," Phoebe replies with a smile.

Back on the *Stellosphere,* Nuala is reunited with her husband.

"Saving Nuala is even better than finding a ghost," says Miles.

"I guess it's time to report back to the admirals that Phantasmos is not haunted," declares Phoebe.

Loretta grins. "Now who's up for hide-and-seek?"